My Little Dinosaur

Written and illustrated by
Ilse-Margret Vogel

gb
GOLDEN PRESS
Western Publishing Company, Inc.
Racine, Wisconsin

I was playing down by the brook one day,
when I found a cave I had never seen before.
And living in that cave was a little dinosaur.

"Hello. Don't be afraid," I said.

And soon he let me pat his head.

A dinosaur is something special to see, and so
I took him home with me.

"We can keep him, can't we?" I said to Daddy.
"He's really very small for a dinosaur."

"Well, I just don't know," Daddy said. "He's rather little now, but when dinosaurs grow, they can get very large, you know. He might get as big as our house someday. Then we wouldn't have a place to stay."

Daddy promised to call a professor he knew.
The professor, he said, might know what to do.

The professor came and looked at my dinosaur.
He said, "This kind of dinosaur doesn't grow.
He will stay the same size always. So I say keep
him. It's unusual today to have a dinosaur.
They're not supposed to exist anymore."

"All right," Daddy said, "he can stay."

So I took my dinosaur to school next day.

Now, I know somewhere there is a rule that says you can't bring a dinosaur to school. But my dinosaur was so polite, the teacher said it was quite all right.

After school it started to rain, and I rode home
on my dinosaur's back.

The people all stopped and stared, amazed.
Some were puzzled. Most were dazed.

You could tell they didn't expect to meet a dinosaur (with a boy on his back) running down the street.

At our door, my dinosaur stopped at the mat and carefully wiped his wet front feet. I thought that was that.

But then what did he do?
He took three steps
forward, smiled at Mother,
and then wiped his back feet, too.

On Saturday we went to Grandmother's house.
She said, "Oh, what a lovely day—with a dinosaur, a boy, and a nice bouquet."
And she brought us
cookies on a tray.

In summer I took my dinosaur to the beach.

He splashed in the surf with my friends and me.

We visited Uncle Fred's farm for a week, and
my dinosaur and I played hide-and-seek.
Where did my dinosaur hide?

I looked all around the barn, front and back,
but I didn't think about the big haystack.

Then I knew that was where he had to be. And
there he was, peeking out at me.

When our cat had kittens, what did my dinosaur do?

He baby-sat for the mother cat.
And seven little kittens got to play with a
dinosaur every day.

When nighttime comes and I go to bed, my
dinosaur lies down by my head. Together we look
at a dinosaur book.

And when I get too sleepy to see, my dinosaur
will turn out the light for me.